Mill Creek Kids

by Colleen Heffernan

illustrated by Sonja Zacharias

All the characters in the story are ficticious.

We acknowedge the support of the Canada Council for the Arts and the Alberta Foundation for the Arts for our publishing program. Thanks to Kim Smith of Priority Printing. A special thanks to Glen Huser who edited all four Hodgepogs and produced the teacher's guides.

Editor: Glen Huser
Production Editor: Peggie Graham
Original book design: Gerry Dotto
Cover art and interior illustrations: Sonja Zacharias
Page set-up and interior design: Chao Yu
In-house co-ordination: Mary Woodbury

A Hodgepog Book for Kids

Published in Canada by Hodgepog Books, an imprint of The Books Collective, 214-21, 10405 Jasper Ave, Edmonton, Alberta, Canada T5J 3S2. Telephone (403)448-0590

Canadian Cataloguing in Publication Data

Heffernan, Colleen, 1959-
Mill Creek Kids

ISBN 1-895836-40-9

I. Edmonton (Alta)-History-Juvenile Fiction. I. Zacharias
Sonja> II. Title
PS8565. E32M54 1997   jC813'.54   C97-910639-7
PZ7.H3584Mi 1997

$\mathscr{D}$EDICATION

The author dedicates this book to her son, Garreth, for his inspiration and to her husband, David, for his support.

$\mathscr{A}$CKNOWLEDGMENTS

The author wishes to thank the staff of the City of Edmonton Archives and Tom Monto of Alhambra Books for their assistance in the research of historical Mill Creek.

Chapter 1

Mess in the Bedroom

Katelyn saw a purple sock peeking out from beneath her bed. She shoved it back under with her foot. Great, she thought, this room is almost ready for mom's inspection. The books are back on the shelf and the floor is clean, except, of course, under the bed.

Katelyn thought her room was dull. Just a bed, a chest of drawers and the closet. A lot of the stuff in the closet wasn't even hers. Like the winter coats nobody wore and her mother's collection of little plastic hangers.

Katelyn wanted to hang pictures on the wall. Her mom said they couldn't put nails in because they were renting this house. Tape, her mom added, might ruin the paint. Katelyn noticed a hook in one corner of the ceiling. Hooks must be different from nails. It gave her an idea.

She dug in a drawer for the ball of yarn they'd bought when she was going to learn to knit. Katelyn had picked the yarn because it was bright and colourful. It started with a strong yellow and then turned into orange, red, brown, red, orange and back to yellow.

Katelyn climbed on her bed and tied one end of the yarn to the curtain rod. She walked across the room and wound it around the bar in her closet. She pulled it tight. She threaded it through the hook in the ceiling and around the knobs on her dresser. Back and forth a couple times between the curtain and the closet and she had her web ready.

Katelyn took a little hanger from the closet and hung it from one strand of the yarn. She taped her latest horse picture to it. There, decoration without nails. A few more hangers, a few more pictures. Katelyn was so busy she didn't hear her mother's footsteps.

The door opened suddenly and knocked several of the hangers to the floor.

"Oh my God, look at this mess. What have you done? You were supposed to be cleaning up and look at this!"

Katelyn's mom grabbed at the yarn and pulled.

"Oh, no, don't do that." Katelyn's warning was too late. The curtain rod came loose and tumbled to the floor. Her mother's face turned pink and her eyes bulged out a little. Katelyn laughed.

"So you think this is funny, do you? Do you?"

"No, yes. It's just..."

"Get out, just get out and let me deal with this mess."

Katelyn picked her way between the yarn and the hangers and ran upstairs to get her coat. As she opened the screen door, she heard her mother call.

"Stay in the yard!"

Chapter 2

Down to the Creek

Thin sheets of ice covered the mud puddles on the street. Katelyn watched a boy at the far end of the block slide his rubber boot onto the ice and step down hard. Crack. Sploosh. Muddy water splashed up over the toe of his purple boot. Some water even splashed over the top of the boot and onto his leg.

"Yes!" he said. Slowly he slid his other boot onto the ice and stepped down hard again. Crack. Sploosh.

"Yes!"

Katelyn watched the boy come down the street. He lifted his boot and stomped, splashing water onto the sidewalk. Then he lifted his other boot and stomped again. He lifted and stomped and splashed all the way down the street.

"What are you doing?" asked Katelyn.

"Breaking the ice," said the boy, "it's fun. There's some left, come and try it."

Katelyn stood on the sidewalk beside the ice. She put one white boot on the ice and stepped down.

"Oohh!" she cried as the ice broke and cold, muddy water splashed all over.

"It's fun, isn't it?" grinned the boy. "I'm Jake. What's your name?"

"Katelyn. You're wearing girl's boots."

"No, I'm not. They're mine." Jake lifted his boot out of the water to show her.

"My mom says that purple boots are for girls. Boy's boots are black."

"Mine aren't. I like purple."

Jake jumped onto the sidewalk beside Katelyn. He turned to face the school across the street. Cupping his hands around his mouth, he hollered, "AAAAEEEEEEEOOOOOOOUUUU!"

It answered back, "AAAAEEEEEEEOOOOOOO UUUU!"

"It echoes," Jake said. "Try it."

Katelyn looked back at her house. Her mom didn't think it was good manners to yell. She cupped her hands like Jake. She called out, not too loudly, "Hello."

There was no answer.

"You have to do it louder," coached Jake.

Katelyn took a deep breath and hollered as loudly as she could, "Hello!"

"Hello!" the echo answered back. Katelyn grinned at Jake. He stuck his fist toward her, his thumb pointing up. "Cool," he said.

"Have you lived here a long time?" Katelyn asked.

"I've always lived here," Jake said.

"We just moved in." Katelyn pointed to their house, the one at the end of the street overlooking the ravine.

"Have you been down to the creek yet?"

"Once," Katelyn said, not adding that her mother had told her never, never to do it again.

"Come on, let's go!" Jake sprinted in his purple boots towards the wooden stairs that went down the hill to the creek. Katelyn only paused a second before she followed him.

Clatter, clatter, thunk, thunk, down they went, their boots banging on the wooden boards. Katelyn ran over to look at a big sign by the bridge that went over the creek.

"What's this?" she asked Jake.

"A map of the park—Mill Creek Ravine Park," he told her. A park, Katelyn thought, her mother might not mind if she went to a park.

"Come on," she waved to Jake as she started across the bridge.

That's when she heard the dog. It was a deep bark. Deep barks usually mean big dogs, Katelyn thought.

Jake looked over his shoulder.

"Where is it?"

"I don't know." Katelyn didn't see the dog until it came around the corner of the house by the creek. When she did, her heart pounded faster. It was a huge black hairy dog, as big as a small horse. And it was coming straight at them.

Jake raced in front of her across the bridge. He tripped and fell just as he got to the other side. Katelyn followed. She had almost reached Jake when

she tripped, landing face down in the dirty snow. Remembering the dog, she covered her head with her arms. But the dog didn't come. In fact, it had stopped barking.

Katelyn sat up. She brushed away the melting snow from her face and looked back. The dog was gone. The bridge was gone. The house was gone and the wooden stairs that led back to their street were gone, too. Only the creek was where it was supposed to be.

Katelyn looked at Jake. He was staring at the creek. "What happened?" she said.

Chapter 3

Where Are We Now?

Jake didn't answer. He just sat staring across the creek. Katelyn shook his shoulder.

"What happened?"

Jake turned slowly to look at her. "I don't know."

"You don't know? You don't know? This was all your idea to come down here and now how are we going to get back? My mom's gonna kill me."

"Hey, don't yell at me. I've been down here a hundred times and this never happened before. It's not my fault."

Katelyn jumped up and brushed off the grit and snow that stuck to her leggings.

"So, where do you think we are, Jake?"

"We're in Mill Creek for sure. That's definitely our hill. A lot of stuff is just missing."

"So where did it go?"

Jake shrugged.

"What's that?" Katelyn pointed to a long wooden building part way up the hill.

"Hey, no fair," Jake said, "they've wrecked our good toboggan run."

"So what's the building?"

"I don't know. I've never seen it before. But I'll never get my snow racer down there now."

"If we don't get home, you'll never ride your snow racer again."

Jake's face turned a little pale.

"Are you scared?" Katelyn asked.

"I'm only scared of one thing."

"What's that?"

"Dogs."

"Oh great! I'd rather be trying to outrun that dog than stuck here not able to get home before mom finds out..."

"Finds out what?"

"Oh, never mind. What are we going to do? How are we going to get home?"

"I think we should go up to that building and see if someone can tell us how to get home," Jake said. "There's smoke coming from the chimney. I bet someone's in there."

"Oh, no," Katelyn said. "We can't do that! I'm not allowed to speak to strangers. Only if they have a

Block Parent sign in the window. I'm staying here."
She folded her arms and kicked at the snowbank.

"I'll go by myself, then."

Katelyn watched Jake climb the hill. She wondered
if she still wanted to stay by herself. She was about to
follow when she saw him twist and fall. He was
holding his hands over his face and moaning.
Katelyn ran up the path.

"What's the matter?" she cried. She smelled the
answer before Jake could tell her. It was a strong, sick
smell. Her stomach churned and she thought she
might lose her breakfast. It was worse than the
outdoor toilet at the lake.

"Phew! yuck!" she called to Jake. "What is that?"

"I don't know. It smells like the lasagna my brother
left in his lunchkit over the holidays. I know one
thing, though."

"What?"

"It's coming from that building."

Chapter 4

A Pair of Brown Boots

Katelyn and Jake sat on the ground waving their hands in front of their noses. Then the wind changed direction and the smell wasn't so strong.

"Let's go," Jake said.

"I don't want to run into that smell again. It makes me sick."

"Just keep waving your hand in front of your nose and it will mix all up."

They climbed the hill together. Jake kicked his purple boots firmly into the snow at each step to keep from slipping. He fanned his face furiously. Katelyn laughed.

"You look funny," she told him. Jake grinned. He scrunched up his nose and crossed his eyes. Katelyn laughed harder. She stood on tiptoe, blinked her eyes quickly and waved her hand as fast as she could.

Jake slipped on the ice. He grabbed Katelyn's jacket to keep from falling. He fell backwards into the bushes along the path. Katelyn's jacket and Katelyn, who was inside her jacket, fell into the bushes too.

"Hey, what'd you do that for?" Katelyn yelled at Jake.

"Sorry, I was just trying to keep from falling."

"It didn't work. Hey, now you've got your elbow in my back."

"No I don't. See!"

Katelyn looked at Jake. His arms were both up in the air, fingers wiggling. She looked down where their boots were jumbled together. There were two white rubber boots. They were hers. There were two purple rubber boots. Those were Jake's. There were two scuffed, brown leather boots. Who did they belong to?

"Hey! What? Who are you?" Katelyn scrambled to her feet faster than she had ever scrambled. She turned to look at the small boy who belonged to the brown boots. He was lying flat, squashed into the bushes. His pants and jacket were dark brown wool. A deep red scarf was wrapped tightly around his neck. A mess of bright orange hair stuck out from under a cloth cap. The hair framed a pair of sky blue eyes that stared up at Katelyn.

"Who are you?" Jake repeated.

There was no answer.

"I'm Jake."

There was still no answer.

"My grandpa has a hat like that," Jake added hopefully. He looked at Katelyn. She shrugged.

"Maybe he can't talk?" Katelyn whispered.

Chapter 5

Davey

Jake stuck out his right hand toward the boy sprawled in the bushes. The boy paused for a second before he grabbed Jake's hand and jumped neatly to his feet.

"I'm Jake," he repeated, "and this is Katelyn. What's your name?"

"Davey," the boy replied. He stared at Katelyn as if she were a new species of bug. Katelyn had seen stares like that before from the Grade Three girl-hating boys. She lifted her shoulders and put her hands on her hips.

"What is your problem?" she asked him.

"My problem is May has taken off. And Vogel's foreman said if he caught her this side of the creek again, he'd butcher her for sure. You haven't seen her, have ya?"

"Who's May?" Katelyn asked.

"Our milk cow."

"Oh, no, we haven't seen a cow." Katelyn looked at Jake for help.

"No cows here," Jake added.

Davey looked puzzled. "And where are ya from?"

"Over there." Jake swung his arm toward the creek.

Davey pulled off his cap and scratched behind one ear. "There's nothing over there but Colonel Stiff's land and our place. Where do ya live?"

"Edmonton," Katelyn jumped in. "We live in Edmonton."

" Ah, well," Davey said. He pointed past the building on the hill. "Edmonton's that way, on the north side of the river. This is Strathcona. No wonder you're dressed queer."

"Queer?" Katelyn looked down at her clothes. She saw pink leggings, white boots and her pink jacket with orange stripes. They did not look queer to her.

"What's that?" Jake pointed to the building on the hill.

"Vogel's," Davey said.

"What's Vogel's?" Jake asked.

"The butchers. Don't you know? Have you not been here before?"

"Uh, not for a long time." Jake pulled at his ear.

"Ah well, that explains it. Vogel only built here a year or two back, just after the century turned."

"Century?" Katelyn's mouth hung open a little.

"Aye. It's 1902 now, you know." Davey laughed and clapped Jake on the back. "But I've got to find May now or my hide'll get tanned. I'm going to circle round behind the pens to see if Vogel's has her."

Davey picked his way down the hill to the creek bed.

"This can't be happening," Katelyn said.

"What did he say? 1902?"

"My mom says this only happens in books."

"It's too weird. Maybe he was joking."

"Then what happened to the bridge? And the dog? And our houses?" Jake didn't answer. They stood quietly for a moment.

"When Alice falls into Wonderland, she finds little packages that say 'Eat Me' and 'Drink Me'. Maybe we should look for some," Katelyn said.

"I think we should go with him. Come on." Jake yelled at Davey to wait and ran down the hill. When he caught up to Davey, he turned and looked back. Katelyn was still standing at the top of the hill, a striped cherry and orange popsicle.

"That brother of yours," Davey told him, "is the queerest boy I've ever seen."

"Where? Where is he?" Jake looked around for a familiar face.

"There, at the top of the hill."

"Brother? Boy? Do you mean Katelyn? She's not a boy, she's a girl."

Davey's blue eyes were as big as saucers.

"No!" he said. "No. A girl? Can't be! She's wearing pants. Queer pants I know, but pants. You let your sister go out wearing pants?"

"Katelyn's not my sister," Jake said. "We're just friends."

Katelyn hadn't moved.

"Hey, Katelyn!" Jake called to her. "Come on. Let's help Davey find his cow."

Chapter 6

A Plan for May

Katelyn vaguely heard Jake call to her. Cow, she thought, what cow? Oh right, the kid Davey had lost his cow. Her mother would be really mad if she went tromping through the creek looking for a cow. Wait, if it was really 1902, her mother wasn't even born yet. Maybe even her grandmother wasn't born yet. Mom couldn't get mad if she wasn't born yet.

Katelyn half skipped, half ran down the hill to the boys.

"He says you're a girl," Davey said, pointing at Jake.

"Oh yeah?" said Katelyn. "So's your mother!" She giggled. Jake giggled. Davey looked puzzled.

"Come on," Katelyn said to Davey. "Where's this cow?"

They scrambled up the bank around the bend in the creek. They stayed carefully behind the brush.

"Phew," Katelyn said, "cow-pies!"

"No," Davey said, "hogs." He parted the bush in

front of them. Long, low fences built into corrals filled the ground below Vogel's building. The animals were hidden, but the smell and the sound of a hundred snuffling pigs filled the air.

"Hey Davey," Jake said, "is that her? Is that May?" Davey followed Jake's finger pointing up the hill. Three men stood by a wooden chute angled down toward the pens. Beside them, tied to a post of the corral, was a soft brown cow.

"Oh no!" Davey groaned. "She's a goner, for sure. That's MacGregor, the foreman. He'll be butchering poor May for Sunday dinner. And mother'll have my hide. I'm dead now, for sure," Davey moaned. He took off his cap and threw it on the ground. He kicked at the bush with his boot. Jake gave a small grin.

"Don't have a cow, man," he said.

Katelyn giggled. Jake giggled. Davey looked puzzled.

"It's okay," Katelyn said, "she's not dead yet. We'll get her back for you. We just need a plan."

"Can you get her home from here?" Jake asked.

Davey scowled at the other two kids. He picked up his cap, slapped it against his thigh and pulled it over his hair.

"Aye, I can ford her across the creek and take her up the path on the other side. But MacGregor isn't going to give her to me. This isn't the first time she's escaped over here. Even if he'd give her to me, I'd have to pay a reward to get her back."

"Well," said Katelyn, "if the men weren't there, you could take her home, right?"

"Aye. But they're not likely to leave any time soon, are they? They're fixing to kill hogs today - and May, too, I reckon."

"Kill hogs? I thought you said it was a butcher shop."

"Aye, but you got to kill them and scald them before you can butcher them."

"Eeouu!" Katelyn wrinkled up her nose, "No wonder it smells like that."

"What would get them away from here for awhile? A fire?" Jake asked.

"You fixing to start a fire?" Davey looked at Jake in horror.

"No. No. What if Katelyn and I circle around and tell them there's a fire? They'll leave and you can get May. They don't know us, so they wouldn't suspect a thing!"

"Well," Davey said, pulling at the peak of his cap, "idea's good, but the fire's wrong. They'd wonder why the fire bell hadn't rung or why you didn't run to the firehall."

"What about a car accident?" Katelyn offered.

"A what?"

"Er, an accident."

"Let me think," Davey said, "My da had a friend just about killed setting the top layer of brick in a kiln. Andersen's brickyard is down the creek on the flats by the river. It might work. It just might."

Chapter 7

Accident at the Brickyard

"Why do we have to go so far?" Katelyn asked.

"Because," Jake said, "we have to look like we've been running a long time. Davey says the brickyard is down by the river. My dad and I ride our bikes down there. It's a long way."

"Well, isn't this far enough?" Katelyn was sure her mother would be looking for her by now.

"Okay." Jake winked at her, "Remember the plan?"

"On your mark. Get set. Go!"

They tore down the path toward Vogel's as fast as they could run in rubber boots. Katelyn's hair was coming loose from her ponytail. It whipped around her face and she brushed it aside so she could see. They started yelling as soon as they saw the building.

"Help! Help!"

The huge man Davey called MacGregor lumbered toward them.

"What's going on?" He scowled underneath shaggy black eyebrows.

Jake stared at the huge man. He looked as if he wanted to speak, but couldn't say the words. Katelyn tugged his sleeve, but he didn't move a muscle.

"They need help at the brickyard," Katelyn said. "There's been an accident and men are hurt."

"Which brickyard?" MacGregor asked.

"Andersen's," Katelyn answered.

"Flynn, Beddard," the man hollered, "come, we must go to Andersen's. There's been an accident." He pointed to Katelyn. "You, run for the firehall. Get more help."

Katelyn paused. She looked at Jake and he looked puzzled, too. The foreman might suspect something if they did not go right away. But which way was the firehall from here? The creek was on their left. The path ran ahead and behind them. Katelyn grabbed Jake's sleeve.

"Come on," she said, and ran down the road to their right.

"Help! Help!" hollered Jake.

Katelyn looked back over her shoulder as she ran. She saw the three men running toward the river. Katelyn didn't feel right about lying to them. She wished there was another way to save May.

Davey watched from the bushes for a long time. He wondered if the strange children were really going to help him. Maybe they had gone home. He was about to make another plan when he saw the foreman walk toward the shop. A minute later, he called the others to join him and left. Davey waited to make sure they were not coming back. Then he scrambled up the hill toward May.

"Whoa, boss." Davey slapped the cow's shoulder and stroked her neck. He lifted the end of the rope off the corral post and led May down the slope to the creek.

May stopped halfway across to take a good, long drink. Davey tugged and tugged on the rope, but May would not move.

"You ornery old cow!" Davey waded back through the water and slapped her rump. "You'd better move, or Vogel's will have your hide and Ma will have mine." May ambled onto the other bank.

Davey looked down at his soggy boots, then back across the creek. Vogel's still looked quiet. There was no sign of Katelyn or Jake, but he had to get May back right now.

"Thanks to ya!" he yelled across the creek.

Potlickers!

"We can stop now. They're gone." Katelyn's feet were getting hot in her boots and the sun was right above them. "What time do you think it is?"

"I don't know," Jake said. "Let's go back and help Davey with the cow."

"It must be almost noon. I've got to get home and we don't even know how! Let's just go. Davey can look after his own cow." Katelyn shook a rock out of one of her boots and eyed Jake carefully. He didn't seem worried about getting home.

"I want to see if Davey got his cow," he said. "There's no hurry about getting home. Maybe we can't get home. Maybe we're stuck here and if we are, we'll need Davey."

Katelyn thought about it. "We've got to get home, Jake."

"Well, all right," Jake said. "I don't think they had television in 1902. My favorite show is on tonight."

"Funnee! Okay, let's go see the cow and then let's go to where the bridge should be. Maybe we can figure out how to get back."

The hogs were still in Vogel's yard, but May and Davey were gone. Katelyn giggled.

"Can you imagine how mad they'll be when they come back and find May gone?"

"No,"Jake said. "How mad will they be when they find out they ran all the way to the brickyard for nothing?"

Katelyn shivered, "That foreman was a scary-looking guy."

"He looked like a shaggy black dog." Jake scrunched his forehead to make his eyebrows look bigger. He put his hands on his hips and stuck his stomach out as far as he could. "What did you do with my cow?" Jake said in a deep voice. Katelyn laughed as Jake strutted around, his legs bowed and his boots splayed out.

"Potlickers!" boomed a big loud voice. They looked up to see the foreman steaming toward them, his face flushed and his arms swinging. Katelyn froze to the ground. Jake shook her arm.

"Come on," he said, "he can't catch us if we run." Jake dragged Katelyn with him for the first few steps until her feet got going. He sprinted around the hill and down toward the creek. Katelyn followed, but her legs felt rubbery like she'd just gotten off a rollercoaster. The foreman was getting closer and he yelled as he ran.

"Scallywags! I'll teach you to play tricks. Bad kids!"

Jake waited for her at the bridge site. He waved his hand toward the other bank. "I don't think we can get back this way," he yelled to Katelyn. The foreman's hand grazed the hood of Katelyn's jacket. She screamed and tried to run faster. Her boots slipped on the wet ground and she slid right into Jake, knocking him over the bank. Katelyn slid right after him toward the cold water.

Oatmeal Chocolate Chunk

Katelyn landed on something hard. Where was the creek? She raised herself on her elbows and turned to look at Jake. He had landed on his hands and knees and was nose to nose with the big black dog that had chased them across the bridge.

"Yip!" The dog made the sound all dogs make when somebody steps on their tail. It tucked its tail between its legs and headed for home, yiping and howling. Jake's eyes were as big as jumbo marshmallows.

"I think I scared him," he said.

"Ah ha," Katelyn sputtered as she started to laugh, "You scared the stuffing out of him. He must have thought you were a ghost. Oh no, it's too funny." Katelyn and Jake held their aching stomachs as they laughed. They rolled on the ground, banging their boots on the bridge deck. A jogger passed by, picking her way gingerly between the two children.

"Hey," Katelyn said, wiping her eyes with her sleeve, "we're home! We're back, back in 1997."

"Yeah, yeah, you're right, we're back, yippee!"

Katelyn grabbed Jake's shoulders and dragged him across the bridge. "We're back, we're back!"

"Kaaatelyn!" A voice wafted down from the top of the ravine.

"What's that?" Jake asked.

"Oh, no! My mom. She'll be mad, we've been gone so long."

"I don't think we have."

"What do you mean? We've been gone for hours."

"Think about it, Katelyn," Jake said. "That dog didn't just sit on the bridge for hours waiting for us to come back. I bet we got back just after he chased us across."

"Well," Katelyn said, "you might be right, but I'm not even supposed to be down in the creek. If I go up the stairs now, she'll know where I've been."

"Oh." Jake thought for a minute. "Come on, I know, let's go up the road." He ran up the road which circled the end of their block. Katelyn followed. At the top, Jake opened a small gate in a white picket fence and went in.

"What are you doing?" Katelyn hissed. She didn't want to be caught in someone else's yard. That was almost as bad as being caught in the creek.

"It's okay," Jake yelled back. "It's my friend, Mrs. Laird."

"Well Jake, how are you today?" An old lady in a pink raincoat was digging in the dirt in the backyard. She was wearing high-top sneakers and thick, blue and white gloves.

"Great, Mrs. Laird. Got any cookies?"

"Now Jake, you know, you have a nose for cookies. I just finished a batch of oatmeal-chocolate chunk this morning."

Jake beamed from ear to ear and his eyes sparkled.

"Oatmeal-chocolate chunk are my favorite," he told Katelyn. Mrs. Laird peeled off her gloves and went into her house.

"I've got to go home," Katelyn whispered.

"Just wait for the cookies. It'll be all right. Wait and see."

Katelyn's mother called for her again just as Mrs. Laird appeared with a plateful of cookies.

"You must be Katelyn," Mrs. Laird said, offering her a cookie.

"Uh, yes, uh, thanks."

"We'd best tell your mom where you are. Yoo-hoo, over here!" Mrs. Laird called to Katelyn's mom.

"Katelyn, I told you to stay in the yard."

"Sorry, Mom."

Mrs. Laird offered a cookie to Katelyn's mom. "My friend Jake here brought Katelyn over to meet the cookie-granny. I hope it's okay if she has one."

Katelyn thought her mom didn't look too mad. She even let her eat two cookies before they left for home.

"Next time," her mom said, "ask first before you go calling on the neighbours."

"I will. I'm sorry for the mess. I just wanted to hang my pictures up."

"Pictures? Was that why you did that?"

"Yeah. You said we couldn't put nails in the wall."

"Right. Maybe there's some other way to do it."

"My teacher uses sticky-tack."

"What's that?"

"It looks like bubble gum, but it doesn't stick to paint. You can get it at the drugstore."

"Really? Well, next time we're there we'll look for it."

Jake hollered from halfway down the block, "Come and play tomorrow. Maybe we'll go see Davey."

Katelyn made a face, but yelled back, "Okay."

"Who's Davey?" her mom asked.

"Oh," Katelyn said, "just a kid we met."

Chapter 10

Wonderbird Park

Jake ran down Katelyn's driveway and stopped at the top of the stairs that led to the creek.

"Hey," Katelyn yelled after him, "you told my mom we were going to Wonderbird Park, not the creek."

"We are going to the park. But the coolest way to get there is through the creek. Come on."

Jake clattered down the stairs. Katelyn followed. This is how we got into trouble last time, she thought. Jake was waiting for her at the bridge.

"Okay," he said, "I'll run across first and see if it works. Then you come, too."

"No way. I'm not getting into trouble again."

Jake paused, "Did you get into trouble?"

"Well, no, not really. But I was lucky. Let's just go to the regular park."

"Come on, it was fun!" Jake poised at the beginning of the bridge, one fist stuck out in front. "To infinity and beyond!" he hollered as he charged across the bridge to the other side.

"Oh, darn, it didn't work," Jake said. He clunked his fist against his forehead and fell backwards onto the ground. He lay there with his tongue hanging out and his eyes fixed on the sky. Katelyn giggled and nudged him with her toe.

"So are we going to this park or what?"

"Sure!" Jake leapt to his feet and set off at a trot. He led Katelyn up the hill and along the trail. Deeper into the woods they went until they reached a dead end at the foot of a large hill.

"Are you sure you know where you're going?" she asked.

"Oh yeah, we just have to climb this hill and there's a path and stairs right to the park."

Katelyn looked at the slope of the hill. It went almost straight up. There were no small trees to hang onto, just a dirt path made slippery by the melting snow.

"It looks steep," she said.

"It's not bad, see?" Jake took a few steps back and took a run at the hill. His boots slipped a little on the mud, but he made it to the top in one try without even putting his hand down for balance. Katelyn was determined to do the same. She took a long run at the hill. She even made it halfway up before she ran out of speed. Her boots started slipping, but she didn't want to put her hand down in the mud and she definitely didn't want to get her clothes dirty.

"Come on," Jake coached, "you can do it!"

Katelyn wasn't so sure. She couldn't seem to get a grip with her boots. She saw a small root sticking out of the hill. She leaned over and grabbed onto it. She squeezed her eyes shut and concentrated on digging into the bank with her toes, but she just slipped further back.

She thought she heard Jake calling from far away. "Katelyn, where are you?"

Chapter 11

A Voice in the Dark

Katelyn opened her eyes. It was dark, so dark she could barely see the hill in front of her. And Jake—where was he? Had he left her here? How did it get dark so fast? How could she get home? She didn't think she could find her way home in the daylight, much less in the dark. Her mom would be past mad, she would be frantic. A small cry of hopelessness escaped her lips.

"Is someone there?" a child's voice asked from somewhere nearby.

"Jake, oh Jake, is that you?" Katelyn cried out.

"No, it is me, Isabelle."

Katelyn's heart sank. Only Jake knew how to get home from here. Although, if she did get home, she might be grounded for life. Maybe she was better off here.

"Can you help me? My foot is stuck." The voice sounded scared, as scared as Katelyn felt.

"Oh, sure. Where are you?"

"Here." Katelyn moved carefully toward the voice. She felt the ground in front of her with the toe of her boot. It was so dark she could only make out vague shapes. One of the shapes moved. Katelyn moved closer and bent down. The girl was a lot smaller than Katelyn. Her dark eyes seemed huge in her pale white face. Her hair was pulled back from her face and covered with a fur hat.

"Where's your foot?"

"At the end of my leg."

Katelyn giggled. "Right!" She touched the girl's leg and followed the thick stocking with her hand. It ended at the ankle. The girl's foot was covered by several heavy stones. Katelyn lifted them up one at a time and heaved them into the blackness.

Bang. Clang. One stone hit something metal. The noise startled Katelyn.

"What's that?"

"The coal pail, I think. Could you get it for me?"

Isabelle sounded so sad that Katelyn stopped heaving stones. She searched with her hands over the mud and rocks until she retrieved a battered metal pail.

"Here it is. I'll put it right beside you."

"Merci, thank you."

"You speak French?"

"Oui."

"I took it in school last year, so I understand a little."

"It is dark, black as coal. Mama will be so worried. I've been trapped here for hours."

"Yeah, me, too. At least, I think so. I was climbing the hill to catch up to Jake. The next thing I knew, it's dark and Jake is gone. Maybe I hit my head and passed out."

Katelyn gave the back of her head a thoughtful rub. No bumps, at least. She lifted the last rock.

"There, can you move it now?"

Isabelle raised her leg and pulled out her foot. She moaned loudly.

"Does it hurt a lot?"

"Oh, oui, it does."

"Let me see." Katelyn knelt beside Isabelle and took the injured foot in her hands. The leather was smooth and soft. The high-top shoe was pointed in the toe. The shoe had little buttons on the side from the toe to the ankle. Best of all, it had a high heel.

"What cool shoes!"

"Cool?"

"Yeah, pretty awesome."

"Oh, pretty, yes. My Tante Hectorine in Montreal. She is very stylish. She gave these to Mama before we left. She said I would grow into them."

"Who gave them to you?"

"My Aunt Hectorine."

"That's a weird name."

"It's the feminine of Hector, the hero, the Prince of Troy."

"Wow."

"I shouldn't even be wearing the shoes. Mama will be so cross. She says they're only for mass on Sunday. But I wanted to see if they fit. I was afraid I'd grow too big and never get a chance to wear them. I didn't have time to take them off before I came to get the coal."

"Are they hard to walk in?" Katelyn had been yelled at more than once for wobbling around in her mother's high heeled shoes.

"They weren't too bad on the flat trail. But it was very hard to climb up to the mine. I think that's why I slipped. Now the coal is all gone and it hurts so much I don't think I can walk home. Mama will be so angry." Isabelle buried her face in her hands and sobbed.

Chapter 12

Peanut Butter in the Dark

Katelyn sat quietly beside Isabelle. They were a pair. Neither one of them could get home and both their mothers would be angry. Wait a minute, she thought, something is weird about this.

"What do you need the coal for?"

Isabelle looked up and wiped her eyes.

"What?"

"What do you need the coal for?"

"For the stove."

"You have a stove that burns coal in the city?"

"The city?"

"Yeah, you know, Edmonton, where we live."

"Oh, I don't live in Edmonton. I live here, in Strathcona."

Katelyn's mind whirled. Where had she heard that before? Of course - from Davey. Now it all made sense.

"And the year, it's 1902, right?"

"Of course."

"Hah, I knew it. Wait 'til I tell Jake I got here all by myself. He'll be jealous." Katelyn jumped up and did a little dance. Isabelle started to cry again.

"What's wrong?" Katelyn asked.

"You are acting so crazy. And I have to get home."

"Oh, I'm sorry. I'll help you." Katelyn turned the pail over and sat down. "What about the coal," she asked, "can we get some more?"

"Not now, it's too dark. And the pick was in the pail so it's gone, too."

"The pick?"

"The pick to chip the coal off with."

"What about the coal you spilled? Maybe we can find it." Katelyn crawled around on her knees, feeling with her hands. "What about this?" She stuck a rock under Isabelle's nose.

"Oh, yes, that's it."

Katelyn collected more rocks, peering at each one carefully before putting it in the pail. "Did you really go down a mine all by yourself and dig out this coal?"

"Yes. It's not down a shaft, just a tunnel. And the coal isn't hard to break off. Mama doesn't like me to do it. She says it's dangerous."

"Why do you do it, then?"

"Papa's had very little work this winter and it helps not to have to buy coal."

"Oh." Katelyn knew what happened when there wasn't enough money to go around. Macaroni a la mode, her mom called it, macaroni and cheese and peanut butter sandwiches.

"Hey, are you hungry?" Katelyn asked.

"Oui, yes."

"I almost forgot—I packed a lunch."

Katelyn dug the food out of her backpack and passed Isabelle a sandwich. Before she could get her own sandwich unwrapped, Isabelle was already finished.

"Here—have this, too."

"No, that's yours."

"It's okay, take it. I'm not that hungry. Besides, there's juice and fruit snacks."

Isabelle chewed the second sandwich slowly.

"This is good," she said, "but it sticks to the top of my mouth."

"Yeah, peanut butter does that."

"What's peanut butter?"

"The brown stuff in the middle."

Katelyn handed Isabelle a juice box. Isabelle looked at it carefully and shrugged. Katelyn took the box, put the straw in and handed it back to Isabelle. She looked at the box carefully and squeezed it. Apple juice squirted all over Isabelle's nose.

"Oh!" she cried, dropping the box.

Katelyn dived to rescue the juice, laughing until her sides hurt. Isabelle laughed too.

"What is it?" Isabelle asked.

"It's a drink, see?" Katelyn said. "Put your mouth over the straw and then squeeze."

Chapter 13

The Mill Creek Mud Monster

The two girls walked slowly along the trail. Katelyn carried the pail in her left hand; her right arm wrapped around Isabelle's waist. The full moon gave them just enough light to see the path.

"Shh," Katelyn said, "listen."

"Gah-lick, gah-lick."

"What's that?" Katelyn whispered.

"Gah-lick, gah-lick."

"Frogs," Isabelle said.

"Oh wow—frogs!"

"You've never heard them before?"

"No—I don't think we have any."

"You don't have..."

"Isabelle!" The voice was faint, but Katelyn thought she saw a light swinging back and forth.

"Mama!"

"Isabelle..." The voice spoke quickly in French. Katelyn couldn't understand everything, but she thought Isabelle's mom was asking where she was. What would her mom be doing now, Katelyn wondered. Would she call the police?

"Listen, Isabelle. I have to go now. My mom will be looking for me, too."

"Oh, of course. But you've never told me your name."

"Katelyn."

"Merci, Katelyn. Merci beaucoup."

Katelyn put the pail down and hurried back along the path. She found herself at the hill. It was still steep and slippery. Somehow I've got to get up this hill, she thought.

She kicked into the clay until she made a small foothold. She hoisted herself upward and flattened her whole body against the hill. The mud was cold on her face as she inched her way up. Her hand felt a root. She tugged to make sure it was sturdy. She scrabbled with her feet and pulled with one hand on the root. She stretched her other arm up, searching for something to hold on to.

A hand grabbed hers and pulled her up. Light blinded her for a second. Then she saw it was Jake.

"You sure are dirty," he said.

Katelyn looked at her clothes. They were caked with brown sticky mud.

"Oh, no! Mom'll kill me."

"It was weird. For a second I thought you'd disappeared."

"I did. I disappeared back into 1902 again."

"No way!"

"Yeah!"

"Darn, double darn, and I missed it. Maybe we can go back right now!" Jake balanced himself with his arms and ran down the bank Katelyn had just climbed.

"Rot, I'm still here." He looked up at Katelyn. "But at least I'm not the Mill Creek Mud Monster." Jake burst into gales of laughter.

"Jake, come on, show me the way home. I can't go to the park like this."

Jake led the way and Katelyn told him all about Isabelle on the way home. They stopped to talk in front of Mrs. Laird's house.

"Could you find that coal mine again?" he asked.

"Maybe we could look for it tomorrow!" Jake yelled, sprinting for home.

"I don't think so!" Katelyn hollered after him. She examined the sleeve of her jacket. Some of the mud was dry and flaking off in small chunks. Oh great, a mud monster with dandruff!

"Oh my, my, whatever happened?" Mrs. Laird poked her head out from behind a bush.

"Gross, eh? Mom's gonna be furious."

"Well, maybe not. Come on in for a bit. Maybe I can help."

Katelyn followed Mrs. Laird into her tiny house. It was clean but cluttered. Every piece of furniture was piled high with books, magazines and other strange things. Mrs. Laird brought Katelyn a laundry basket and a fuzzy pink sweatsuit.

"Here, my dear. You can change in the washroom and I'll ask your mom if you may stay for tea."

Soon Katelyn was happily dunking shortbread cookies into a steaming mug of tea.

"Wherever did you find that much mud, my dear?"

"In the creek by the coal mine."

"Coal mine? You mean the old Twin City Mine?"

"I...I don't know."

"Did you see the mine?"

"No, but Isabelle said it was there."

"Oh, I see. There was a mine in the creek. But I'm sure you couldn't find a trace of it now. Let me show you."

Mrs. Laird dug out a book from one of the piles and opened it to a map.

"The ground, you see, is like a big birthday cake. It's put down in layers: a layer of cake, then pudding, then more cake, raspberry jam, more cake and so on, with the icing on top. The coal seam is like a layer of pudding."

"Only not as tasty."

"Right. Edmonton has three big seams. The one at the surface is called the Weaver and two farther down named Clover Bar and Lower."

"Three layers of pudding, yum."

"The first coal mines were drift mines to collect the top layer of coal. The miners would find the seam

of coal along a bank and pick away at it until it was too dangerous to work."

"Why was it dangerous?"

"The miners didn't put supports along the walls or the ceiling of the tunnel. That meant it could collapse at any time."

"Oh no!" Katelyn thought about Isabelle collecting coal. If the tunnel caved in, no one would even know she was there.

"This star on the map shows the Twin City Mine in Mill Creek, but you can't find it anymore. Lord knows, I walked long miles with my husband trying to find it. He was an amateur historian. He always said, 'How can you know where you are if you don't know where you've been?'"

Katelyn shook her head. "I don't understand."

Mrs. Laird laughed and offered Katelyn another cookie.

Chapter 14

The E Y and P

Jake hopped on one foot back and forth across Katelyn's driveway.

"What are you doing?"

"Hopping on orange leaves and waiting for you."

"Orange leaves?"

"You know:

Step on yellow—holler and bellow,
Step on red—you'll wind up dead,
Step on green—let out a scream,
Step on orange and eat ice cream."

"Orange doesn't rhyme with ice cream."

"Yeah, but I love ice cream. What took you so long?"

"I had to clean my room before I came."

"Yuck, I like my room messy. Come on, Mrs. Laird's waiting."

"At least we don't have to sneak down to the creek today."

"Do you think we'll find anything?" Jake's eyes gleamed with anticipation.

"No way! We spent the whole summer trying to find a coal mine or another way to go back to see Davey and Isabelle. And what did we find? Nothing. So today we're going to find...uh...hi Mrs. Laird. What are we going to find today?"

"The first bridge across Mill Creek—the railway bridge on the E, Y & P."

"What's the E, Y & P?" Jake asked.

"The Edmonton, Yukon and Pacific Railway. It was a little railway with big ambitions. When it started, they were going to lay track thousands of miles to the gold fields of Dawson City, Yukon. But they only got as far as Edmonton."

"Where did they start?"

"In Strathcona."

"But that's just across the river."

"I know, I know," Mrs. Laird chuckled. "They fell a bit short, didn't they?"

Katelyn, Jake and Mrs. Laird took the steps down to the creek and climbed the hill on the other side. Mrs. Laird pointed along the wide, paved trail. "This was the track for the E Y & P. We're going to follow it south to where the bridge crossed Mill Creek Ravine.

In the other direction, the railway crossed the river to Edmonton."

"Past Vogel's."

"Why Katelyn, that's right! Vogel's abattoir used to stand right at the top of this hill. How ever did you know that?"

As they ambled along behind Mrs. Laird, Katelyn's mind raced to think of an answer. She didn't think Mrs. Laird would believe in time travel.

"Hey!" Jake shouted. "She's gone—disappeared."

Katelyn looked—he was right. Mrs. Laird had vanished into thin air.

"It's not fair," Jake complained, "Everybody gets to go but me."

"No, Jake, look." Katelyn bent down and touched the shiny metal rail. "It's us that's disappeared."

Chapter 15

A Problem for Four

The train tracks ran past Vogel's Meat & Packing Co.. A small boy climbed up the hill from the creek, a package in one hand and a cap on his head. Small tufts of orange hair stuck out from underneath the cap. Jake punched Katelyn in the arm.

"Hey, it's him. It's Davey! Hey, Davey!"

The boy turned toward them and pulled on the peak of his cap.

"Good morning to ya," Davey said as Jake and Katelyn ran up to him. "I haven't seen ya since spring."

"How's May?" Katelyn asked.

"Ornery as ever, thanks to you." Davey grinned. "I'm off to Vogel's with butter for Mr. MacGregor. Do ya want to come?"

Katelyn shivered at the thought of the huge man with the shaggy black eyebrows.

"We'll wait here for you, Davey," Jake told him.

Katelyn sat on the dried grass beside the tracks. Jake practiced handstands.

"Don't fall onto the tracks. A train might be coming."

"Naw," Jake said, jumping lightly to his feet. "Nothing coming but Little Red Riding Hood."

"What?" Katelyn squinted in the direction Jake pointed. There was someone coming wearing a red cape and carrying a basket. Katelyn thought she looked familiar.

"Isabelle? Hey, Isabelle, it's me, Katelyn."

Isabelle caught up with them just as Davey dashed out of Vogel's to join them. Katelyn introduced Isabelle to the two boys.

"So what are you doing with the basket," asked Jake, "taking cookies to granny's house?"

"Granny? No. I am taking dinner to my papa. He is working for the railroad now, just south of here."

"Can we come along?" Katelyn asked.

"Sure, why not?"

Jake and Davey ran ahead. The girls put the basket between them and carried it together.

"I'm so glad you're okay," Katelyn said. "Mrs. Laird says the coal mine tunnels can collapse on you."

"Oh? Well, Papa is working now, but..."

"Promise me you won't do it again? Okay? I don't want anything to happen to you."

"All right, I promise."

"That's a great cape."

"Oh, oui. Tante Hectorine sent it from Montreal. She thinks this is a very wild place to live, so she sends us the latest fashions from Quebec."

"Cool."

"No, it is wool, very warm."

"No, I meant it's neat."

"Ah, oui, neat and tidy."

"Oh, well, actually..."

"Hey, hey, come here, quick," Jake called to them. "We found a dead guy on the tracks."

A large, heavy man lay sprawled across the tracks. Davey knelt beside him and touched his forehead.

"Is he really dead?" Katelyn asked.

"I don't think so," Davey said. "He's still warm."

Isabelle bent down toward the man and sniffed.

"Whiskey," she said. "My Uncle Raymond smells like that on Christmas Eve."

"We've got to get him off the tracks," Katelyn said. "What if a train comes?"

"Maybe we can wake him up," Jake offered. He yelled, "Hey, wake up!" and shook the man's shoulder. The man just lay there.

"Let's pull him off the track, then," Jake said. Each of them grabbed part of an arm and heaved and pulled. "All together!"

"It's no use," Davey said. "He must weigh twenty stone."

"I bet Mr. MacGregor could lift him. Let's go get him, Davey." Katelyn looked back at Jake and Isabelle. "Keep watching for trains!"

Two men were talking to Mr. MacGregor as the kids burst in.

"Mr. MacGregor, come and help. There's a man lying across the tracks."

"Dead, is he?" chuckled Mr. MacGregor to the other two men.

"No sir, dead drunk."

"Really?" Mr. MacGregor began, then he spied Katelyn. "Well, you thought I'd forgotten you, did you? Thought you could play another trick like the last time? Get out, Davey Donnell, and take your friend with you. Or it'll take more than butter to keep your hide from being tanned."

Davey took off his cap on the front step and slapped it hard against his leg.

"Gods o' war!" he said.

"What?" Katelyn asked.

"It's what Da says when he's real mad." Davey pulled his cap over his hair and gave the peak a sharp tug.

"I shouldn't have come," Katelyn said. "He might have believed you if I wasn't there."

"Nah, he's like that. So what are we going to do now?"

"Let's roll him over and then try to pull him off the tracks. How often do trains come?"

"Four times a day. But Da says you never know when a train is going to come. The train from Calgary is sometimes a full day late. He sings this song whenever Ma wants him to go meet the train:

'The C & E why bless your heart,
the Catch—me—Easy line
That never broke its record yet
by coming in on time.'"

"We'd better run."

Chapter 16

Mill Creek Kids

Jake sat cross-legged beside the man on the tracks. He tickled the man's nose and moustache with a stalk of timothy.

"I don't know," he said to Isabelle, "I think this guy is dead. Even my dad wakes up when I do this to him."

"Did you hear something?"

"No, what?"

"There it is again," Isabelle whispered. "My God, it's a whistle, a train whistle."

Katelyn knew something was wrong when she saw Jake standing perfectly still.

"What is it?" she yelled.

Jake pointed south along the track.

Isabelle hollered, "The train!"

"Oh no," Katelyn said, "we've got to stop it!" But how? It was like a huge black animal charging along the tracks toward them. Of course, she thought, Isabelle's cape!

"Quick, take that off," Katelyn said.

Isabelle's eyes grew wide as Katelyn tugged at the fasteners on her coat. "What are you doing?"

"We'll flag the train with it."

Isabelle swung the cape off her shoulders and started to run toward the train. Katelyn, Davey and Jake ran with her, yelling and waving their arms. As the train got closer, it blew a loud whistle.

"Stop!" Katelyn yelled, but she didn't think anyone could hear above the screech of the train. The huge black engine, puffing and smoking, came closer and closer. Jake yanked her arm and pulled her off the tracks. Isabelle and Davey came with them.

They watched as the train moved slowly past them. It ground to a halt just before it reached the man on the tracks.

"Whew!" Davey wiped his sleeve across his forehead.

"Hooray, we did it!" Jake yelled.

"You are the bravest person I know," Katelyn told Isabelle.

"Not so brave."

"We're all heroes now," Davey said.

"Yeah, maybe we'll be on TV," Jake said.

"What?"

"You know, on the news."

"Oh, the newspaper. Maybe. Here comes Mr. MacGregor. I bet he's sore he didn't believe us."

"I don't like him when he's angry," Katelyn said. "Let's get out of here."

"Oh, Papa's dinner, I forgot!"

Isabelle collected her basket and they walked together beside the tracks. Katelyn looked back. The men from the train and the men from Vogel's talked loudly, waving their arms. One of them pointed at the kids. Another yelled, "Hey you!"

A strong, burning smell passed along the top of Katelyn's throat and then it was gone. Katelyn stumbled and a cyclist whizzed by in front of her nose.

"Do be careful, my dear." Mrs. Laird put a hand on Katelyn's arm.

"Oh darn," Katelyn whispered to Jake. "Darn, double darn, we never ever get to say good-bye."

"Yeah, bummer," Jake said.

Jake stomped the first snow of the year off his boots and rang Katelyn's doorbell. He paused. He rang the bell again.

"Hi, can Katelyn come out to play?" he asked her mom.

"If she's finished with her room, she can. Katelyn, Jake's here."

Katelyn appeared at the bottom of the basement

stairs. "Come on down. There's something I want to show you."

"What? Your clean room?"

Katelyn stuck her tongue out at Jake. "It's cool, I promise."

Jake clattered down the stairs and followed Katelyn along the hall.

"Oh, no," he said. "It's too clean. Aaargh, no, let me out!"

"Now close your eyes."

"Aw geez."

Katelyn smiled. She pulled off bits of blue sticky tack from the package on her bed. She stuck the big picture to the wall above her bed. A huge, black train engine puffed and steamed. Four kids stood in front and waved. One wore a red cape.

"Okay, open your eyes."

"Cool. That's us. Did you paint that all by yourself?"

"Sure," Katelyn said. "You want to hear something spooky? I thought I heard a train whistle last night."

"Oh yeah, we hear those all the time. Dad says they're from the rail yards in Old Strathcona. Sometimes we can even hear the freight cars banging together."

"Oh darn, I was hoping it was a ghost. Mrs. Laird says real artists name their paintings. What do you think I should call this one?"

"Hmm." Jake thought for a minute. "How about,

Godzilla meets the Mill Creek Kids?"

"Godzilla! You watch too many monster movies!"

"Well, Mr. MacGregor kind of reminded me of Godzilla."

Katelyn laughed. She looked at the picture. Hmm, she thought, Mill Creek Kids, I kind of like that!

ABOUT THE AUTHOR

COLLEEN HEFFERNAN was born and grew up in the Lesser Slave Lake region of Alberta. She studied Journalism and English Literature at Carleton University, Ottawa. The mother of three sons, she is active in her children's school and contributes volunteer time in-class and with school council. She is currently working on an anthology of short fiction for young adults and a juvenile novel. *Mill Creek Kids* is her first published work.

ABOUT THE ILLUSTRATOR

SONJA ZACHARIAS lives in Red Deer, Alberta and has a B.A. in drama from Augustana University College, Camrose. She has designed and constructed costumes for the Camrose Scandinavian Theatre Festival and the Rosebud School of the Arts. and now works primarily as an artist. Her watercolours are in private collections in Alberta and British Columbia. *Mill Creek Kids* is her first book project.

A teacher's guide for Mill Creek Kids is available from Hodgepog Books.